animals**animals**

Rats

by **Renee C. Rebman**

Marshall Cavendish
Benchmark

New York

Special thanks to Donald E. Moore III, associate director of animal care at the Smithsonian Institution's National Zoo, for his expert reading of this manuscript.

Library of Congress Cataloging-in-Publication Data
Rebman, Renie C., 1961-
Rats / by Renee C. Rebman.
p. cm. — (Animals animals)
Summary: "Provides comprehensive information on the anatomy, special skills, habitats, and diet of rats"—Provided by publisher.
Includes index.
ISBN 978-0-7614-4877-8 (print)
ISBN 978-1-60870-619-8 (ebook)
1. Rats—Juvenile literature. I. Title.
QL737.R666R43 2012
599.35—dc22
2010016034

Photo research by Joan Meisel

Cover photo: Hugh Willcox/Getty Images

The photographs in this book are used by permission and through the courtesy of:
Alamy: Tony Hobbs, 17; Wesley Roberts, 26; Kevin Webb, 27; Wildlife GmbH, 32; imagebroker, 34; blickwinkel, 37; *Corbis*: W. Perry Conway, 25; Michael Freeman, 30; James L Amos, 38; *Getty Images*: GK Hart/Vikki Hart, 1; DEA/A. Jemolo, 7; John Downer, 8; David J. Sams, 14; *Photo Researchers Inc.*: Stephen Dalton, 18; *Photolibrary*: G. Delpho, 10; C. Sanchez, 12; Gerhard Schulz, 13; J-P. Ferrero & J-M. Labat, 22, 33; Regis Cavignaux, 28; *SuperStock*: age fotostock, 4; All Canada Photos, 20.

Editor: Joy Bean
Publisher: Michelle Bisson
Art Director: Anahid Hamparian
Series Designer: Adam Mietlowski

Printed in Malaysia (T)
1 3 5 6 4 2

Contents

1 Historically Unwelcome

Night falls in the city. The brown rat scampers quickly through the dirty wet sewer. It pops up through a small hole in the grate and travels down a dark alley. It slithers against the rough bricks of the buildings, using the *guide hairs* on its body to feel its way. Climbing up into a smelly dumpster located behind a restaurant, the rat easily gnaws a hole through a full garbage bag and begins to eat. There is a shuffling sound as other rats drop into the dumpster. It is a favorite place to dine for this rat family. All over the city rats are making their way through the streets to search for food left behind by humans. It is a behavior that has been repeated daily for thousands of years.

Rats are intelligent, alert, and always on the lookout for their next meal.

Ancestors of rats appeared on Earth 57 million years ago. Scientists know this from finding fossilized rat remains in droppings from *predators* that ate them. These *rodents* were strong survivors. Their numbers grew over millions of years.

Rats lived among the earliest human communities. Skeletal remains of rats have been found in caves of prehistoric hunters dating back 30,000 years. Rats stuck close to humans for one reason—to eat their food. This is known as *commensalism*, which means one *species* benefits from the other without harming it. Rats did not directly harm humans, but they certainly became terrible pests.

In ancient Egypt, people ate a lot of grain, which they stored in large containers. Rats looked for meals in the containers and consumed the food. The problem became so widespread that the Egyptians looked for ways to get rid of rats. They left food out to attract cats and encouraged them to live in their cities. The cats helped get rid of the rats and were soon admired by the Egyptians so much that they made laws to protect them. Egyptians even had a goddess named Bast who was depicted having the head of a cat. People loved cats and despised rats.

Rats originated in Asia and made their way to other parts of the world on trading ships. Ship rats lived below-decks in the bottoms of the ships and survived off the food stored for the sailors. Once a ship landed in a port to trade and sell merchandise, the rats would come ashore. No matter where they landed they were unwelcome guests. Rats destroyed food that was stored for humans and invaded their homes.

In the year 1348, rats brought the terrible bubonic *plague* to Europe. The plague killed more than 25 million people. It wiped out an estimated 50 to 80 percent of the population. The bubonic plague was known as the Black Death.

Ancient Egyptians loved cats and often depicted them in their artwork.

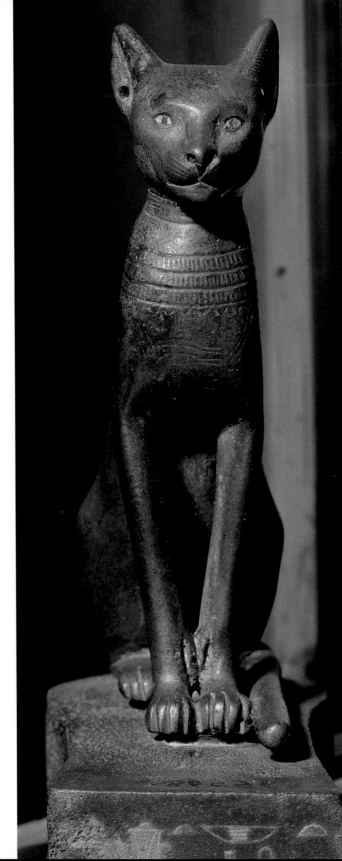

These rats are stealing grain stored for humans.

No one knew for certain what caused the disease. Some blamed the rats. In fact, it was the fleas that lived on the rats that transmitted the disease. Fleas would bite rats and pick up *bacteria* that was present in their blood. The fleas would jump from rats onto humans and bite them, spreading the plague.

The plague finally subsided by 1350 but reoccurred from time to time well into the 1600s. No one knows the reasons the plague stopped and started. It may be that better hygiene ultimately ended plague epidemics.

Rats came to the United States with the first settlers on the ships that arrived from Europe. Millions of rats live in this country today. They are still pests but are not considered a public health hazard. Although thousands of people get bitten each year, rat bites are less risky than dog bites, which can transmit rabies.

Many people fear and despise rats. They are unpopular but fascinating animals.

Did You Know . . .
The bubonic plague still exists today. There are about ten to twenty cases of the plague reported in the United States each year. Modern antibiotics can cure an infected person if administered in time. If not, the disease is fatal.

Anatomy of a Rat

There are two types of common rats that live among us: the brown rat and the black rat. These names are deceiving because either type of rat may be any color from black to brown, gray, or white. Anyone seeing a rat knows for certain what it is, but there are a few small differences between the two types.

The black rat is also known as the roof rat because it is an excellent climber. It is smaller in size than the brown rat. The roof rat is slimmer in shape than the brown rat and has a pointy snout.

The brown rat is also known as the Norway rat or sewer rat. No one is certain how the Norway rat got its name as it certainly did not come from Norway.

This brown rat is demonstrating its agility as it climbs down a slender pipe.

Species Chart

There are more than fifty species of rats in the world, but the two most widespread species are the black rat and the brown rat.

◆ The black rat is also known as the roof rat and usually lives high off the ground, such as on the roof of a building. Its body is around 8 inches (20 centimeters) long, and it weighs 7 ounces (200 grams). Its thin tail is a little longer than its body.

The roof rat is easily spotted by its large ears and long tail.

The brown rat weighs twice as much as a roof rat.

◆ The brown rat is also known as the Norway rat or the sewer rat. It grows to about 12 inches (30 cm) in length and weighs about 14 ounces (400 g). It has smaller ears and a shorter tail than a roof rat. It also can be more aggressive.

A rat's incisors are very strong and can bite through many different materials.

They are popularly known as sewer rats because they hang around in sewers. While there are a few differences between Norway and roof rats, they have very much in common.

One of the most distinctive features in rats (and all rodents) is their front teeth, or *incisors*, which are large and amazingly strong. A rat can gnaw through just about anything—from glass, to brick, to wood. All that gnawing helps keep its teeth short. A rat's incisors continue to grow throughout its lifetime at the rate of about 5 inches (13 cm) per year. If a rat did not wear down its teeth to a reasonable length by gnawing on objects, the teeth could lock together and the rat would starve to death. This could happen because a rat's incisors grow at an angle. If gnawing did not wear them away, the upper incisors would curl sharply backward and lock up with the lower incisors, which would curl upward. This would prevent the animal from eating. A rat with long curling incisors cannot bite or chew.

Rats have three types of bites. A rat has a bite it uses for feeding. It uses a different bite for gnawing. When chewing on something such as wood, a natural protective action occurs. A membrane slides down between the incisors that prevents the rat from swallowing anything harmful. A rat biting in self-defense or during an attack separates its incisors to create a larger and more harmful bite than the feeding or gnawing bite.

Rats have a terrific sense of balance that is helped by their long tails. They can run along fence tops, thin pipes, and even clotheslines without falling. If a rat begins to fall, it can grasp a nearby object with its tail for support. Rats grab onto objects by curling their tails around the object, similar to how a monkey does, but the rat's grasp is not as strong.

It will also use its tail while swimming, holding it up out of the water for balance. Rats can swim a distance of 0.5 miles (0.8 kilometers) without stopping and are able to tread water for three days if necessary. A rat can also hold its breath for three minutes. It is easy to see why rats are so at home in sewers.

Rats have great endurance and a lot of strength for such small animals. Their leg muscles are so strong a rat can jump 3 feet (1 meter) straight up in the air or leap across a distance of 8 feet (2.4 m). During short bursts of running they can reach an amazing speed of 24 miles (39 km) an hour.

They are also experts at climbing. Their front and back paws have four main digits

Did You Know . . .
Rats keep their teeth sharp by grinding the bottom incisors against their upper incisors. This is called bruxing. One of their jaw muscles runs through the eye sockets behind their eyeballs. During bruxing, this muscle causes the eyes to vibrate. A rat sharpening its teeth can look pretty scary when its eyes vibrate.

This rat runs quickly along a slender rope using its tail for balance.

with curved claws and a small, nearly useless thumb. Rats use their claws to hang onto surfaces, to *groom* themselves, and to pick up their food to eat. Rats usually sit up on their rear paws and hold their food in their front paws to dine.

Rats have strong leg muscles and can jump across distances as wide as 8 feet.

Their flexible skeleton is another amazing rat feature that comes in handy. Rats are actually able to collapse their rib cages. That is why a rat can get through any opening its head will fit through. It can squeeze through a hole the size of a quarter.

Rats have poor eyesight during the day and can not see beyond about 4 feet (1.2 m), but have very good night vision. They are color blind and see objects as black, gray, and white. Their other senses—hearing, touch, and smell—are all highly developed. They use these senses, rather than sight, to find food. In fact, their sense of smell is as well developed as that of a dog. Their hearing is also excellent, and a rat will swivel its ears to detect the origin of a sound just like a cat would. It can detect sounds that are too high-pitched for a human to hear.

Their long facial whiskers and guide hairs on their bodies help them sense their surroundings. Their sense of touch gives them security and a sense of direction. That is why rats prefer to stay close to walls as they move around rather than dart across an empty room.

A rat's sense of taste is very important. It helps the rat avoid poisons. If a rat tastes something wrong with its food, it will urinate on it. This keeps other rats from eating it. If any rat sees another rat fall ill or die after eating, it will avoid that food. Rats do not have the ability to vomit, so eating anything poisonous is likely to kill them. Rats are clever and are built for survival.

3 Daily Life of a Rat

Rats live anywhere humans live except in the very cold regions near the North and South Poles. Norway rats are found in great numbers in the United States, Canada, and Europe. Roof rats are more commonly found in the southern part of the United States, in Central, and South America, as well as in the parts of Europe and Africa that border the Mediterranean Sea.

Rats are social creatures and prefer to live in a group. Roof rats are true to their name and will build their nests in attics of buildings or in nearby trees. Norway rats live in basements, sewers, along riverbanks, or underground.

Rats hold their food in their claws while eating.

Several rats stay warm and cozy in this chamber of a burrow.

When living underground, rats will construct *burrows* about 18 inches (46 cm) below the surface of the ground. These burrows are mazes of numerous chambers connected by a system of tunnels. The burrows are built near a source of food, such as a city dump or a farm with food storage for livestock in barns and outbuildings.

The main entrance is a very small hole about 2 to 3 inches (5 to 7 cm) across. Rats will often try to seal the entrance by covering it with dirt or leaves. They do this for safety and to keep out the weather.

The tunnels lead to chambers that vary in size. A chamber may be small and accommodate one or two rats, or maybe a mother and her babies. Chambers may also be large and accommodate between several rats and dozens of them. Male rats usually live in separate burrows, except in large *colonies*. In larger colonies, males may live in the same burrow, but they live in chambers that are separate from females. When a rat colony increases in number, more chambers are added to the burrow.

The living chambers are filled with bits of rags, dried vegetation, leaves, or other materials to make it comfortable. Not all chambers contain rats. Some are used for food storage. Others may be filled with grain that the rats urinate on. Once the mixture of grain and urine begins to *ferment* (break down and cause gases to form) it will generate heat that will keep the burrow warm.

Burrows are always constructed with one or more holes called bolt holes in the back areas away from the main entrance. These allow the rats to make a quick escape if a predator tries to enter the burrow.

Living in such close quarters does not bother rats. They generally get along quite well together and enjoy snuggling close and grooming each other. When a large number of rats live together, some males may occasionally display aggression to try and win a dominant place in the pack.

To display dominance, a rat may gnash its teeth, arch its back, or throw dirt backward with its hind feet. It may also run head on toward another rat in an outright attack. Rats also rise up on their hind legs and push at each other with their forepaws in a boxing manner. They also jump at each other and sometimes wrestle on the ground. The rat retreating first is the loser. The largest and toughest rats soon become the most dominant.

Communication among rats is important. Rats make high-pitched sounds that humans cannot hear but that other rats can hear up to 50 feet (15 m) away. Rats will warn each other of danger or share information about a food source.

Rats are *nocturnal* and spend most of the night searching for food. A rat must eat one-tenth of its body weight each day in order to survive. It will hunt for its food alone, traveling up to 0.25 miles (0.4 km) at a time.

Did You Know . . .
Rats are surprisingly caring to members of their specific family or other members of their pack. They have been observed feeding sick or handicapped rats. Blind rats will hang on to the tails of seeing rats and allow themselves to be led through tunnels.

Albino rats have white fur and pale pink eyes due to their lack of pigment.

During one night, a rat can log more than 1.5 miles (2.4 km) during its travels.

Rats are *omnivores*. This means they will eat almost anything. Their diet consists mainly of vegetables, fruits, and nuts, but they will eat insects, eggs, and meat, and nearly anything else they can scavenge. Rats do not just gulp down their food. Instead, they pick out their favorite morsels to enjoy first.

Rats eat dessert first, choosing to nibble on their favorite foods immediately during a meal.

Once the rat finds food, it will usually take it back to its nest to eat in safety. If the food is too large for one rat to move, another rat or two will help drag the feast home. Rats generally hunt for food on their own but do communicate with others in their family if they find a large food source and need help transporting a big piece of food. When they discover a good food

26

source such as a garbage dump, rats will visit it again and again. They are also thirsty animals and must consume 0.5 to 1 ounce (0.03 to 0.06 pints) of water daily.

Searching for food and water is a big task for the rat. After a long night of hunting for nourishment, rats return to the safety of their nests and sleep the day away.

Water is a very important part of a rats daily diet.

The Life Cycle of a Rat

Rats multiply at an amazing rate. Female Norway rats are ready to become mothers at around three months of age. They have no particular mating season and will mate all year round. Female roof rats begin to mate at four months of age and usually mate in the summer.

When a female rat is ready to mate, her body produces *pheromones*. These pheromones produce an odor that attracts males. The odor is detected by the male rat's *vomeronasal organ*. She will mate with several rats, to ensure that she becomes pregnant. During mating the male rat will make a singing sound that is too high-pitched for a human to hear. After mating, male rats have nothing to do with the female.

Rats can give birth to up to twelve pups in one litter.

She will be responsible for raising her *litter*.

The gestation period for a rat is only twenty-two to twenty-four days. While she is waiting to give birth she prepares her nest. Norway rat mothers have individual nests within a burrow. A roof rat will find a private space in a wall or attic to make her nest. A female roof rat will have about six to ten pups per litter. Norway rats have slightly larger litters of up to twelve pups.

After giving birth, rats are able to become pregnant again within hours. Females can produce as many as seven litters per year. One single female rat can have around eighty pups per year. This incredible capacity to breed makes certain the world will always be populated with rats.

Tiny helpless newborn rat pups weigh only one-fifth of an ounce.

Newborn pups are born blind, hairless, and completely helpless. They are tiny, weighing 0.2 ounces (5 grams). The mother rat will gently lick the babies to clean them and get them moving. She will *nurse* them and watch over them. If her pups are threatened by any predators or an invading male rat, she will fight fiercely to protect them. She will leave the nest only for short periods of time to find food for herself. Other female rats from the burrow may also help watch over the young pups if necessary and keep them safe from male rats. In this nurturing environment, pups grow and develop quickly.

After only eight days the newborn pups grow fur. By two weeks their eyes open, and they can begin to explore away from their nest. They must stay close to their mother or risk great danger from predators. Rats have natural predators such as dogs, cats, hawks, owls, snakes, skunks, and raccoons. These animals quickly recognize young rats as easy prey and take them for a tasty dinner.

At three weeks of age the young rats are *weaned* from their mother and no longer need her milk for nourishment. They wander out on their own to scavenge for food.

After eight days a newborn rat will develop fur.

When young rats are not feeding, they spend their time playing with their many siblings. Rats chase each other, wrestle, and box, mimicking behavior they see in older rats. They do not fight with older rats for fear of getting hurt, and older rats instinctively leave them alone to grow up in peace.

Once young rats are ready to live on their own, the young male rats will leave the female burrow and find another burrow with other male rats. Female rats may stay within the burrow, establishing their own nests and having pups of their own.

Rats do not have easy lives. They face a constant struggle to find food. Younger and

Rats make excellent mothers and take very good care of their young.

weaker rats are likely to die if there is a shortage of food. Older and stronger members of the rat pack take the food for themselves and in extreme cases of starvation will turn on the weak rats and eat them. Rats also face illness, accidents, and poisons. Most rats will not live to see their first birthday. Some rats can live up to three years in the wild, but the majority of rats have a shorter life span.

5 The Positive Side of Rats

While the majority of people dislike and fear rats, there are many who keep them as pets. Pet rats are known as fancy rats. They have been specifically bred as pets for more than 150 years. Rats first began to be taken in as pets in the 1840s.

Queen Victoria of England had her own royal rat catcher named Jack Black, who kept the rat population under control in the palace. He became very interested in the rats. When he saw rats with unusual coloring, he kept them and began to breed them. He soon had rats that were *albino*, gray, fawn, and multicolored. Ladies in the royal court began to keep the rats in cages as pets. Even the queen kept a few pet rats. Black began to sell them to other rich women in

Many people enjoy keeping "fancy" rats as pets.

London, who were thrilled to have the same type of exotic rats as the queen. Rats became popular pets.

After more than 170 years of breeding, fancy rats are now quite unusual. They come in even more distinct colors such as yellow, cinnamon, silver gray, and blue gray. Some are multicolored and/or have a stripe down their backs. Some fancy rats can have soft sleek fur while others have curly coats. Pet rats, like their wild cousins, like grooming themselves.

Pet rats are not as aggressive as wild rats and enjoy their human companions. Male pet rats make good lap animals and like to cuddle and be petted. Female pet rats tend to need more active play. Pet rats are very social and like to have other pet rats as company. It is a good idea to have at least two pet rats. Make certain both rats are the same sex or you will soon have baby rats. With good care, fancy rats can live two to three years—plenty of time to provide a lot of entertainment and affection.

Rats can also provide more than affection to humans. Laboratory rats are crucial to medical research. Lab rats have been in use in the United States for more than one hundred years. There are now around three hundred private companies that

Pet rats are very sociable and enjoy cuddling with their owners.

This albino lab rat is being studied for scientific research.

breed and supply rats meant for research. More than 20 million lab rats and mice are used in the United States per year.

Like fancy rats, lab rats have been bred to be suitable for specific uses in a lab. Some rats have identical *genetic* makeup. This is accomplished through inbreeding—continually breeding rats from the same family. Other rats are bred with rats from different families and have a different genetic makeup. Because rats reproduce so quickly, scientists can study their offspring as well. This helps when scientists are trying to determine how certain diseases or conditions are handed down through generations in a human family.

Most lab rats are albino, but other types are also used. Rats suffer from many of the same ailments and diseases as humans such as high blood pressure, diabetes, cancer, and Alzheimer's disease. Testing rats that have these conditions helps scientists find new medicines and treatments. Many new drugs and medicines are tested on lab rats.

In the early 1950s Dr. Jonas Salk used lab rats while he was developing a vaccine for polio.

Did You Know . . .
Rats often accompanied astronauts on the space shuttle. Rats are being studied to help scientists understand the effects of weightlessness on the body. Scientists study rats' brains to detect any structural changes experienced during space flight. The changes the rats experience are probably also experienced by human astronauts.

This disease crippled thousands of people and was sometimes fatal. Today, the disease is on the verge of being wiped out due to Salk's vaccine.

Scientists also used lab rats to discover how to keep the body from rejecting internal organ transplants. When a person receives a new kidney, for example, it is crucial that the kidney thrives and functions in its new body. Rats were injected with many different antirejection drugs until a successful one was found.

Cancer research has been conducted on rats for years. By exposing rats to cigarette smoke, scientists proved tobacco use causes cancer. By implanting cancer cells in rats, scientists can study how the disease spreads and test drugs that may stop it.

Lab rats are now being used to study spinal cord injuries. Scientists are developing methods that enable rats with spinal cord injuries to walk again. One method involves implanting a computer chip into the rat's brain that sends signals to the muscles telling them to move. Some of these methods are now being used on humans.

Some people feel using lab rats, or any animal, for scientific experimentation is cruel. Yet many life-changing, and even life-saving, medicines have been developed due to this type of testing. In many ways, rats serve humans well and improve our lives.

Glossary

albino—A mammal lacking color in the skin, hair, and eyes.

bacteria—Microscopic organisms some of which produce disease.

burrow—Underground hole made by an animal.

colony—A group of animals that live together.

commensalism—One species benefiting from another without harming it.

ferment—Chemical breakdown of an organic substance.

genetic—Relating to heredity, family members have the same genetic makeup.

groom—To clean hair or fur.

guide hairs—Hairs on a rat's body that rub against surrounding objects and aid the rat's sense of direction.

incisors—Front teeth adapted for cutting and gnawing.

litter—Young animals born together.

nocturnal—An animal that is mainly active at night.

nurse—Act of young getting milk from its mother.

omnivore—An animal that eats both plants and meat.

pheromone—Chemical substance produced by an animal that provokes a response in another animal.

plague—A destructive contagious bacterial disease.

predator—An animal that hunts and kills other animals for food.

rodents—Animals with front teeth especially adapted for gnawing.

species—A classification of an animal or plant.

vomeronasal (Jacobsen's organ)—An organ that produces pheromones in certain mammals.

wean—To accustom young to eating food rather than nursing.

Find Out More

Books

Day, Trevor. *The Secret Life of Rats: Rise of the Rodents*. Mankato, MN: Coughlin Publishing, 2009.

Markle, Sandra. *Outside and Inside Rats and Mice*. New York: Simon & Schuster, 2009.

Marrin, Albert. *Oh, Rats!* New York: Dutton Children's Books, 2006.

Savage, Stephen. *Rat* (Animal Neighbors). New York: PowerKids Press, 2009.

Whitehouse, Patricia. *Rats* (What's Awake?). New York: Heinemann, 2009.

Websites

Interesting Rat Facts
http://wererat.net/ratfacts.htm

More Rat Facts
http://hubpages.com/hub/Interesting-Facts-About-Rats

Pest World for Kids
www.pestworldforkids.org/rats.html

Pet Rats and Mice
www.afrma.org/rminfo1.htm

Index

Page numbers for illustrations are in **boldface**.

About the Author

Renee C. Rebman has published more than a dozen nonfiction books for young readers. Her Marshall Cavendish titles include *Anteaters, Turtles and Tortoises, Cows, Cats, How Do Tornadoes Form*, and others. She is also a published playwright. Her plays have been produced in schools and community theaters across the country.